בס"ד
לד' הארץ ומלואה

This book belongs to:

Hachai

Please read it to me!

Let's
Go to Shul

written and illustrated by
Rikki Benenfeld

Hachai
PUBLISHING

Let's Go to Shul

First Edition
April 2002 / Nissan 5762

Sixth Impression
September 2014 / Elul 5774

In Honor of the
Bar Mitzvah of my son, Uri

In Honor of all my
children who inspire me
(Even when they tire me!)
Thank you Devorah, Roslie,
Tzipora, Aharon and
Yocheved. R.B.

Editor: Devorah Leah Rosenfeld
Layout: Eli Chaikin

ISBN 13: 978-1-929628-08-7
ISBN 10: 1-929628-08-0
LCCN: 2001098185

HACHAI PUBLISHING
Brooklyn, New York
Tel 718-633-0100 Fax 718-633-0103
www.hachai.com – info@hachai.com

Printed in China

On Shabbos morning, I can't wait,
It's time for Shul – let's not be late!

My Shabbos shirt is stiff and white,

My shiny shoes are buckled tight.
Let's go to Shul!

I love to walk to Shul, don't you?
The grass is green, the sky so blue!

I always think of things to say
As we hold hands along the way.
Let's go to Shul!

Kiss the Mezuza carefully,
And come inside my Shul with me!

I'm quiet as a baby bird,
I don't make noise or say a word,
When I'm in Shul!

Next to Mother, over there,
A Siddur's waiting by my chair.

My father's Tallis looks so fine,
The Chazzan davens line by line.

I can daven; I can sing,

And thank Hashem for everything,
When I'm in Shul!

The Ner Tamid,
A special light,
Is always lit
And burning bright.

The Aron Kodesh opens wide,
I see the Torah right inside,
When I'm in Shul!

The Rabbi lifts the Torah high,
I kiss it as it passes by.

The Bimah's where we read and roll,
The Parsha from the Torah Scroll.

I hear Kiddush, then I take,

Some grape juice and a piece of cake.

A lollipop, so sticky-sweet

Is my favorite Shabbos treat!

I say, "Good Shabbos,"
to my friend,

I can't wait to come back again...

...right back to Shul!

Glossary

Aron Kodesh	Holy Ark
Bimah	Platform on which the Torah is read
Chazzan	Cantor; one who leads the prayers
Daven	Pray
Hashem	G-d
Kiddush	Blessing over wine recited on Shabbos and Festivals
Mezuzah	Parchment scroll inscribed with hand-written text of Shema, affixed to the doorposts of a Jewish home or building
Ner Tamid	Eternal Light
Shabbos	Sabbath
Shul	Synagogue
Siddur	Prayer book
Tallis	Prayer shawl
Torah	Handwritten parchment scroll containing the Five Books of Moses

Other titles in the
Toddler Experience Series:

COLLECT THEM ALL!

Let's Go to the **Farm**

written and illustrated by Rikki Benenfeld

Let's Meet **Community Helpers**

written and illustrated by Rikki Benenfeld

Let's Go **Shopping**

written and illustrated by Rikki Benenfeld

I Go to the **Dentist**

written and illustrated by Rikki Benenfeld

I Go to a **Wedding**

written and illustrated by **Rikki Benenfeld**

I Go **Visiting**

written and illustrated by Rikki Benenfeld

I Go to the **Doctor**

written and illustrated by Rikki Benenfeld

I Go to **School**

written and illustrated by Rikki Benenfeld